The Flowering Cross

A Faith Imprint™ Book

Placing God's Truths in the Hearts of Children

by Beth Ryan

Illustrated by
Renee Graef

NASHVILLE   DALLAS   MEXICO CITY   RIO DE JANEIRO

To my precious children who reveal God's love
to me in amazing ways every day. And to my
mother who instilled in me a fervency for the
things of God since childhood.

© 2009 by Beth Ryan

Illustrations © 2009 by Renee Graef

All rights reserved. No portion of this book may be reproduced, stored in a retrieval system,
or transmitted in any form or by any means—electronic or mechanical, photocopy, recording,
scanning, or other—except for brief quotations in critical reviews or articles, without the prior
written permission of the publisher.

Published in Nashville, Tennessee, by Tommy Nelson. Tommy Nelson is a trademark of Thomas
Nelson, Inc.

Thomas Nelson, Inc., titles may be purchased in bulk for educational, business, fund-raising, or
sales promotional use. For information, please e-mail SpecialMarkets@ThomasNelson.com.

Scripture quotations are taken from *The Holy Bible, International Children's Bible.* © 1986, 1988, 1999
by Thomas Nelson, Inc.

Library of Congress Cataloging-in-Publication Data

Ryan, Beth, 1957–
    The flowering cross / written by Beth Ryan ; illustrated by Renee Graef.
      p. cm.
    Summary: Neighbor Papa Jack has a surprise for six-year-old Katie, after she picks the
prettiest flowers from his garden for the Flowering of the Cross ritual at her church's annual
Easter service.
    ISBN 978-1-4003-1537-6 (hardback) [1. Easter—Fiction. 2. Neighbors—Fiction. 3.
Flowers—Fiction. 4. Friendship—Fiction.
5. Church—Fiction. 6. Christian life—Fiction.] I. Graef, Renee, ill. II. Title.
    PZ7.R94765Fl 2010
    [E] —dc22
                            2009034194

mfgr. RR Donnelley
Shenzhen, China
10/09 – PPO #99789

Dear Parents,

Inspired by the book *Won by Love*, which reveals how God used a seven-year-old girl to win the heart of Norma McCorvey (Jane Roe of *Roe v. Wade*), *The Flowering Cross* is a testimony of how a child can influence an adult for Christ. The simple faith of children, accompanied by pure motives, often breaks through barriers that adults simply cannot. *The Flowering Cross* shows children that they too can win others for Christ.

The Faith Imprint™ found on the bottom of the pages throughout the book presents an opportunity for you to teach your children about Jesus and place His truths on their hearts. Where you see a Faith Imprint™ take a moment to share with your child the Scripture verse and what it means.

Also, I encourage you to create a special Easter tradition by using a cross like the one at the back of the book. Bring family and friends together to celebrate, and invite each of them to place a flower in the cross while expressing thanks to Jesus for something specific in their life.

Beth Lyan

A bright ray of sunshine peeked between the curtains and shone right on Katie's face. Outside the birds sang a cheery wake-up song.

Katie's eyes popped open, and she sat straight up in bed as she remembered this was a special day. "It's Easter!" she said to the birds and the sun, and to her puppy, Waggles.

Faith Imprint: Share what the first Easter was like when Jesus overcame death.

"You are looking for Jesus from Nazareth, the one who was killed on a cross. He has risen from death."

(MARK 16:6)

"Katie," Mommy called out from the kitchen. "Hurry and get your bath so you can go to Papa Jack's to pick your Easter flowers."

Katie threw back the covers and leaped out of bed, leaving Waggles in his favorite spot.

Faith Imprint: Share how Katie did what her mother told her to do.

"Children, obey your parents the way the Lord wants. This is the right thing to do."
(Ephesians 6:1)

Papa Jack was their next-door neighbor.
He grew the most beautiful flowers in town.
And today Katie would pick his prettiest
flowers for the Flowering of the Cross.
Katie was one of the few who dared
to step foot in Papa Jack's garden.
Around town, he was called Mean
Old Jack—better known for his ill
temper than his beautiful flowers.
Balls and kites that landed in his
yard were abandoned because no
one was brave enough to retrieve
them from his yard.

Katie's mommy said their grouchy neighbor just needed an extra dose of kindness and love. So whenever she made homemade pies, she took one to him. When a big storm blew limbs all over his yard, Nolan, Katie's eight-year-old big brother (whom Katie called NoNo), and their daddy helped pick them up. When Mr. Jack was sick, Mommy was there with hot soup. Each time, Katie went too, bringing her bright smiles and pictures of flowers to share.

Even Mean Old Jack couldn't resist such kindness for long. Soon Katie and NoNo were welcome visitors to his garden. And Mean Old Jack became Papa Jack to them.

Faith Imprint: Share how Katie's family loved their neighbor.

Jesus said, "'Love your neighbor as you love yourself.'"
(MATTHEW 19:19)

Katie pulled back the shower curtain and let out such a squeal of happy delight that Waggles ran to see what had caused all the fuss. There hidden in the bathtub was the prettiest Easter basket ever.

Katie carefully examined each treasure in her basket, but she quickly forgot about the candy and the pretty cross necklace when a pink Bible caught her eye. It was her first big-girl Bible, and she would take it to church, along with Papa Jack's flowers. And maybe, just maybe, this would be the day Papa Jack would go too.

Faith Imprint: Share how Jesus wants us to have joy in our life.

"I came to give life—life in all its fullness."
(JOHN 10:10)

Mommy often invited Papa Jack to go to church with them, and Katie had done the same. But he never went to church, not even on Easter Sunday. At first his answer had been a gruff, "No." The next time, it was simply, "Not today." Then more recently it was a thoughtful, "Perhaps another time."

When Katie reached Papa Jack's house, she knocked softly on the door.

"Good morning, Katie. You look like one of my prize spring daffodils," he said. But what Papa Jack said next was a big surprise. "Katie, today I'm going to church with you."

When she heard this, Katie was so happy, she almost forgot the flowers she'd come to pick.

"You may select any flowers you like," Papa Jack said, spreading his arms wide to indicate anything in his garden. Katie chose pretty pink tulips and bright yellow daffodils.

Mommy, Daddy, and NoNo were already in the car, but Katie and Papa Jack decided to walk the two blocks to church. On the way Katie began to tell him all about the Flowering of the Cross.

"Jesus is God's Son," she told Papa Jack. "But some mean people nailed Him to a cross. He died so that we could go to heaven with Him one day." Then Katie explained, "Jesus' friends buried Him in a tomb, but God made Him come back to life again."

Faith Imprint: Share how Jesus willingly gave His life to take our place.

"The Son of Man must be given to evil men, be killed on a cross, and rise from death on the third day."

(LUKE 24:7)

"Mommy says Jesus loves me so much that He died for me," Katie said. "And when I put flowers on the cross, it's a way of saying thank you to Jesus for all He has done for me."

"Papa Jack, aren't you glad Jesus loves you?" Katie waited for his answer, but Papa Jack was silent.

"Here," Katie said, offering him a pink tulip. "You can put one on the cross too." Papa Jack took the flower in his rough hand and looked away before Katie could see the tear that slid down his cheek.

Faith Imprint: God loves each of us very much.

"For God loved the world so much that he gave his only Son. God gave his Son so that whoever believes in him may not be lost, but have eternal life."

(JOHN 3:16)

During the service, the pastor shared how much God loves us, and Papa Jack thought of all the kindness Katie and her family had shown him, even when he didn't deserve it. Now he knew God's love was even greater than that.

When the pastor finished speaking, it was time for all the children to go forward for the Flowering of the Cross.

Katie gently took Papa Jack's rough hand in hers and led him straight to the cross.

Katie placed her flower near the bottom of the cross, while Papa Jack placed his near the top. Seeing this, Katie quickly pulled her flower out and whispered, "Pick me up so I can put mine next to yours."

Papa Jack's heart was filled with love for the first time—love for a little girl and for the Savior that she had shown him. As he lifted Katie up to place her flower next to his, Katie exclaimed, "Thank you, Jesus!"

"Amen!" boomed the voice of Papa Jack, as he joined in Katie's praise to Jesus.

"Papa Jack, please come to our house for Easter dinner," Katie begged on the way back home.

"And then we can go fly my new kite!" chimed in NoNo.

"I would like that," Papa Jack answered. "But first I need to stop by my woodshop for a bit."

Later at home when NoNo saw Papa Jack heading to the woodshop, he was right behind him. While Katie got to help Papa Jack in the flower garden, NoNo was always at his side in the woodshop.

Faith Imprint: Share with your child how joyful it is to fellowship with other believers.

"They broke bread in their homes, happy to share their food with joyful hearts."
(ACTS 2:46)

Katie peered out the window, waiting for NoNo and Papa Jack. At last, she saw them coming and ran to meet them at the door, wondering what NoNo carried in his hands.

"Look what we made!" NoNo proudly said. "It's a flowering cross without the flowers." And it did look just like the cross at church, only smaller.

"NoNo's right," said Papa Jack, "we need some flowers for it. Let's go see what we can find."

Some of the other children from the neighborhood were playing outside. "Come pick some flowers," Papa Jack invited. At first, the children eyed him suspiciously, but his broad smile and Katie's and NoNo's welcoming waves soon won them over.

No one knew at the time, but this was the beginning of what would become a neighborhood tradition—Easter flower picking in Papa Jack's beautiful garden.

Faith Imprint: Share how God's love can change anyone.

"If anyone belongs to Christ, then he is made new. The old things have gone; everything is made new!"

(2 Corinthians 5:17)

Easter dinner with Katie and her family was another tradition that Papa Jack looked forward to for years to come. And every year, the Flowering Cross stood in the center of the table, covered with his most spectacular flowers.

For Papa Jack, it would always be a beautiful reminder of how a little girl led him right to the cross and Jesus' amazing love.

Faith Imprint: Talk about how even children can share their faith in Jesus with others.

"I thank you, Father, Lord of heaven and earth, because you have hidden these things from the people who are wise and smart. But you have shown them to those who are like little children."

(LUKE 10:21)

Photo used by permission
of P. Graham Dunn

Have Your Own Flowering Cross Celebration

Bring your family and friends together to focus on Jesus, thanking Him for His wonderful love demonstrated to us at the Cross.

Directions for grownups to make a Flowering Cross*

Step 1—Obtain one piece of wood that measures at least 8" x 18" (you will need to cut the cross and the base from this piece of wood). A piece of 1" x 10" pine or white wood from any home improvement center will work.

Step 2—Cut out the base by cutting a piece of wood that measures 4" x 4".

Step 3—Draw the cross on a 7½" wide x 12" tall piece of wood using the measurements on the blueprint.

Step 4—Cut out the cross along the lines drawn in Step 3. (A jigsaw, band saw, scroll saw, or handsaw will work.)

Step 5—Drill holes in the cross.

Step 6—Drill a hole in the center of the base for the screw to go through, and drill a pilot hole a little smaller than the screw you are going to use in the bottom of the cross.

Step 7—Glue or screw the base to the cross.

Step 8—Sand the cross and base so it is smooth.

Step 9—Stain or paint cross.

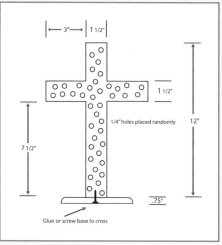

Directions by Jim Liddle

* Note to Parents: These instructions are for adults with woodworking experience and not intended for children.